SOLOMON GRUNDY

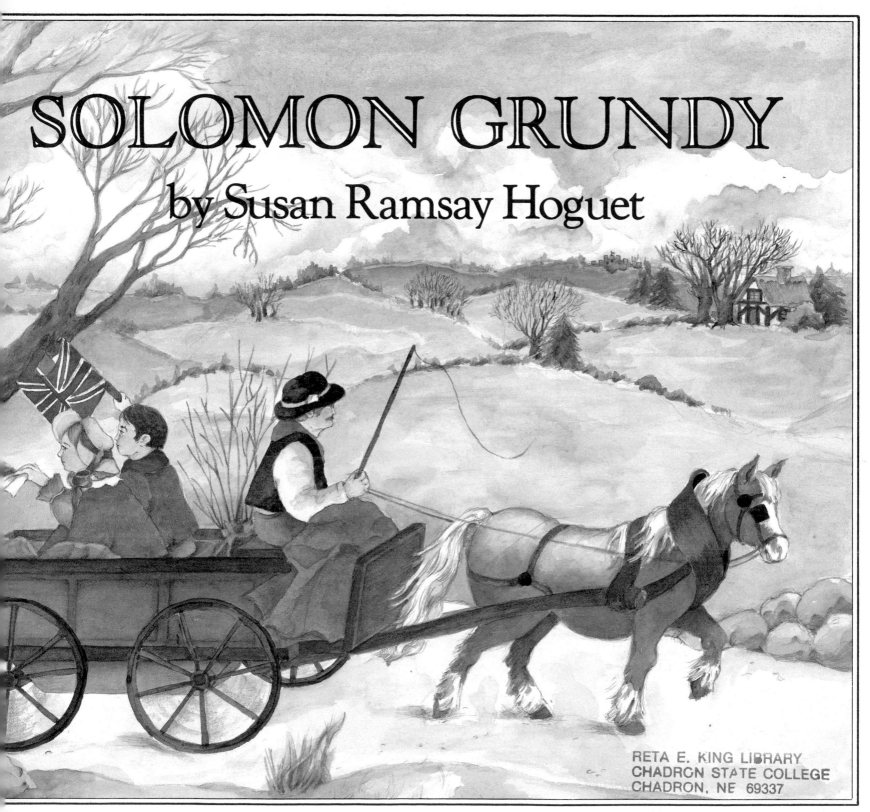

SOLOMON GRUNDY

by Susan Ramsay Hoguet

E. P. DUTTON   NEW YORK

for Marty Gilbert
with many thanks to Winston

Copyright © 1986 by Susan Ramsay Hoguet

Library of Congress Cataloging in Publication Data

Hoguet, Susan Ramsay.
Solomon Grundy.
Summary: The author creates her own Solomon Grundy,
child of English immigrants to the United States, who
lives a pleasant life as a baker in nineteenth-century
Connecticut. Includes the original nursery rhyme.
[1. United States—Social life and customs—19th
century—Fiction.   2. United States—Social life and
customs—1865–1918—Fiction.   3. Bakers and bakeries—
Fiction.   4. Nursery rhymes]   I. Title.
PZ7.H6847So   1986   [E]   85-20453
ISBN 0-525-44239-1

Published in the United States by E. P. Dutton,
2 Park Avenue, New York, N.Y. 10016
Published simultaneously in Canada by
Fitzhenry & Whiteside Limited, Toronto

Editor: Ann Durell   Designer: Edith T. Weinberg
Printed in Hong Kong by South China Printing Co.
First Edition   COBE   10 9 8 7 6 5 4 3 2 1

7

9

Solomon Grundy, born on a Monday

christened on Tuesday

married on Wednesday

took ill on Thursday

FUNDS NEEDED
TO FINISH STATUE'S BASE

worse on Friday

died on Saturday

buried on Sunday.

The gravestone reads:

PAX

Solomon

July 4, 1836

Sept. 24, 1910

This is the end of Solomon Grundy.

About the Book

SUSAN HOGUET created her own Solomon Grundy for this book and made him a part of the growth of America. Solomon is imaginary, but the details of his background are authentic and based on careful research in source material such as newspapers and fashion books of the times, and old prints and photographs.

pages 6–7: Solomon's parents emigrate from Liverpool, England. They arrive in New York, after a voyage of forty days, on March 13, 1830.

page 9: They buy a farmhouse in Connecticut.

page 10: They plant saplings brought from England in the apple orchard beside the house.

page 11: Solomon is born July 4, 1836.

page 17: In 1860, Solomon marries Deborah, a girl he has known since they were christened together.

page 18: Solomon and Deborah have four children: two boys and two girls.

page 19: They start baking and selling pies made from their apples.

page 20: In 1870, they open the Grundy Bakery in Connecticut.

pages 22–23: Solomon holds a pie-eating contest at the Philadelphia Centennial Exposition, 1876, to help raise money for the pedestal of the Statue of Liberty.

pages 26–27: The bakery business is expanded to New York City, 1890.

page 28: Solomon and Deborah have a 50th wedding anniversary party in 1910.

page 29: Solomon dies on September 24, 1910. He is much mourned by his family, especially his two oldest grandchildren.

page 30: He is buried near the church in which he was christened.